For Joseph, my best friend
—A. Y. L.

To my grandson, Burhan Hitz
—Demi

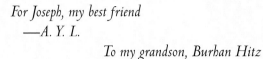

Wisdom Tales is an imprint of World Wisdom, Inc.

LIBRARY OF CONGRESS CATALOGING-IN-PUBLICATION DATA

Lumbard, Alexis York, 1981-
 Conference of the birds / retold by Alexis York Lumbard ; illustrated by Demi ; foreword by Seyyed Hossein Nasr.
  p. cm.
 Based on a thirteenth-century Sufi parable by Attar.
 ISBN 978-1-937786-02-1 (casebound : alk. paper)
 I. Demi. II. 'Attar, Farid al-Din, d. ca. 1230. Mantiq al-tayr. III. Title.
 PZ7.L978714Co 2012
 [E]--dc23

2012008103

The illustrations are rendered in mixed media.

Book design by Michael Nelson.

Printed in China on acid-free paper.

Production Date: April, 2012

Plant & Location: Printed by Everbest Printing (Guangzhou, China), Co. Ltd / Job: #105012

For information address Wisdom Tales, P.O. Box 2682, Bloomington, Indiana 47402-2682

www.wisdomtalespress.com

The Conference of the Birds

RETOLD BY
Alexis York Lumbard

FOREWORD BY
Seyyed Hossein Nasr

ILLUSTRATED BY
Demi

Wisdom Tales

Birds, their flight, and their wings are universal symbols of the spirit and of spiritual journeying. This can be seen in cultures as diverse as the Egyptian, ancient Persian, Greek, Christian, and Islamic. It was in fact Plato who said that the wing of a bird is the most apt symbol for the spirit. The Quran also speaks of "the language of the birds," meaning a language conveying a secret spiritual message revealed by God to Solomon.

There are many important literary works of Persian Sufi poetry which deal with birds and their flight as symbols of the life of the spirit and of spiritual wayfaring. This poetry (based both on the Quran and on Islamic cosmology) concerns the cosmic mountain on whose peak presides the mythical bird Simurgh, whose name and imagery were drawn from earlier Zoroastrian sources. The most outstanding of these works is the *Mantiq al-Tayr* (translated usually as *The Conference of the Birds*) by Farid al-Din Attar, the 12th century Persian poet who is one of the greatest figures in the history of Sufi poetry and one of the main inspirations of Rumi. A poem in rhyming couplets or the *mathnawi* form, this work of over 4,000 verses is considered by the most knowledgeable authorities to be one of the supreme masterpieces of Sufi poetry and in fact of mystical literature considered globally.

Like so many other Sufi literary works and especially poetry, Attar's masterpiece has the power to speak to both the advanced pilgrim upon the spiritual path and the simple believer. In Persia its verses are discussed assiduously by accomplished scholars, but they are also cited from memory by simple bakers and cobblers who may even be illiterate. Attar's work has been a source of inspiration and emulation by many a later writer not only in Persia itself but also in Muslim India and the Ottoman world. In Persian it has also been adopted into simpler versions for the young. Moreover, ever since its composition, the *Mantiq al-Tayr* has inspired numerous painters and its scenes have been depicted in numerous masterly miniatures, especially Persian ones. The present book is a very successful endeavor of this kind.

This book, which is tailored to young readers, is special because the adaptor of the text, like one of the birds in the story, is in the process of "taking flight" to seek spiritual knowledge, and she brings this experience to her work; at the same time, being the mother of three children, she has direct experience with the developmental and spiritual needs of the young. Her literary efforts are complemented in this volume by the remarkable illustrations of Demi. In our times, most paintings that are considered modern or postmodern represent what is, in fact, "sub-real." Demi, however, creates paintings that possess a traditional character and they depict a world which is spiritual in nature and which stands *above* the ordinary world that surrounds us, not below it. Her paintings draw from the vision of the celestial world, rather than from an artist's lower psyche. When one beholds the images of the birds she has painted for this volume, one is reminded of the depiction of animals in classical Chinese and Japanese art or in classical Persian miniatures.

The collaboration of these two gifted women is indeed felicitous. Together they have created a precious work which enables the young to enter a world of truth and beauty that is denied to them in so much that they read and see today. I congratulate both Alexis York Lumbard and Demi for producing this wonderful book, and hope and pray that it will reach as wide an audience as possible.

—SEYYED HOSSEIN NASR

ate one moonless night
in a far corner of the world
there gathered a large flock
of birds. They gathered in sorrow,
since they had been, for so very
long, deprived of a king. No king
to uphold the law. No king to
keep the peace. No king to share
the wisdom. A hush came over the
crowd when the bird with black-
tipped feathers on her head and
a sacred prayer inscribed upon
her beak stepped forward:

"My feathered friends, do not despair,
I know you feel alone.
But rise and cheer, we have a King!
I've seen His golden throne.

"He waits for you, my feathered friends,
Our King Simorgh the Wise.
With Him you'll find a love that's true,
A love that never dies.

"And though the quest is long and hard,
You'll never be the same.
Commit yourselves to finding Him,
There is no better aim."

The birds flapped their wings
with uncontrollable joy. "Please,"
they begged, "Please, O honorable
hoopoe, take us to our King!"

Just as the birds were about to leave, the duck hesitated: "I care not for long trips. I am quite happy in my pond. Perhaps I'll go another night."

"But don't you know that tomorrow
May never come your way?
And is your life in this small pond
As merry as you say?

"So do not let this laziness
Destroy this golden chance.
Release its hold upon you now,
And to your King advance!"

The duck stared at the reflection of clouds sailing in the still waters of his pond. Even the clouds seemed to advance with purpose. "What if the hoopoe is right?" he pondered, "a chance like this, a chance to meet a loving, majestic King. I have to go. I must go. I must go now!"

So, all the birds, duck included, set off upon their journey.

After some time, the parrot, weighed down with heavy jewels and jewelry, slowed her pace. She soon stopped altogether. "I cannot fly any more, I am far too tired," she panted.

"Dearest friend, you'll fly like the wind,
With strength and ease and more.
Just put aside those chains of gold
And let your spirit soar!

"Soar on to the King, the crown jewel,
And then you'll truly see
That nothing is as beautiful
As His grand Majesty.

"So do not let rich attachments
Destroy this golden chance.
Release their hold upon you now,
And to your King advance!"

The parrot looked to the path ahead: "Is our King truly as beautiful as you say?" "Yes," the hoopoe nodded. The parrot's eyes sparkled like never before. She ripped off her heavy jewels and gems and threw them on to the ground. "Then there is no time to waste. Here I come, my King, here I come," and she fluttered off like a love-struck fledgling.

The flock arrived at a tall and ancient forest. Off in the near distance a storm was brewing. As the skies grew darker the tiny finch trembled with a mighty fear. "Sorry master, but I cannot go any farther. I'll never make it through the thunder and lightning."

The owl, who stared relentlessly at the poor little finch, let out a cruel snicker.

The hoopoe stepped forward:

"No, do not laugh, do not condemn
When others fail or fall.
There is a weakness to be found
Hidden inside us all."

"Brother finch," said the owl,
"I am so sorry. Fear not, fear not."

The hoopoe smiled and wrapped
her wing around the finch:

"Deep in the darkness of the storm
Heaven will see you through,
We all have the strength we need
Including little you!

"You must make a firm decision
To conquer all that fright.
By finding faith and courage now,
The end will be in sight.

"So do not let your many doubts
Destroy this golden chance.
Release their hold upon you now,
And to your King advance!"

In an explosion of courage,
the finch hurled himself straight
into the dark, menacing clouds.
The others watched as strong gusts
of wind tossed the finch's tiny body
from side to side but still he kept
going. The others quickly followed.

It had been many days since the flock first began their journey. They had endured countless miles of strange and unknown valleys, survived the heat of scorching hot deserts, and now, perched upon a large tree at the edge of a shore, the birds rested. Stretched out before their eyes was a seemingly endless ocean, and somewhere, in that vast ocean was an island. Atop the island's one and only mountain, presided King Simorgh.

"How much farther must we go?"
complained the partridge.

The hoopoe answered:

"Those of us who've learned to endure
 With hopeful, bright smiles,
Will have the strength to handle now
 A thousand more miles.

"They know with every hardship,
Greater is the reward.
Focus your mind upon this truth
And you shall see your Lord.

"So do not let this impatience
Destroy this golden chance.
Release its hold upon you now,
And to your King advance!"

The partridge closed his eyes. "Simorgh, Simorgh, Simorgh!" he said, repeating the King's name over and again. When he opened his eyes, he saw ahead not the journey's length, but the journey's end. With the thought of the King ever present, the partridge flew onward.

The skies were bright and the water
below sparkled like liquid turquoise.
The birds were getting closer to
the holy island. Some thought they
could see it. Some thought they
could feel it. Others just waited.

And then, far off in the horizon, they caught their first glimpse.

Just then the hawk shot ahead, disappearing into a thick band of mist.

The mist grew heavier and heavier and it soon clouded over the sky in every direction. This worried the hawk greatly. He could no longer see the island of King Simorgh. "Am I going the right way?" he thought.

Confused, he flew faster and faster, and the faster he flew the more desperate he became. And then he stopped. He stopped panicking. He stopped struggling. He let go of all his desires to be the very first bird to meet the King, and hovered in mid-air. The hawk turned to the heavens and wept: "Forgive me. I have made a terrible mistake. Without you, I am lost," and he prepared himself for certain death.

And then out of the mist the
hoopoe emerged,

"We all must learn to lose ourselves
    To be what we must be.
  You've passed the great and final test
    And learned humility.

"You've cast away your foolish pride,
Which is the King's behest.
And so my dear pure-hearted friends,
Let us conclude our quest."

Like curtains on a stage, the mist parted. With lowered heads and racing hearts, the birds completed their journey.

At the top of the sacred mountain there stood no throne, no King, just a simple lake surrounded by eternal snow. One by one the birds approached the water's edge. As each of the birds stared down at their own reflection, the hoopoe began her final speech:

"I know that you came here thinking
You'd meet a birdlike King.
But the King I have brought you to
Is not an earthly thing.

"He's the King of all the heavens
And all found here below.
To Him, your hearts are like this lake
Reflecting in His glow.

"But none of us could ever see
His light of truth within,
Unless the mirror of the heart
Is free of dust and sin.

"And now that every one of us
Has shed sin's mighty hold
Of inner faults and outer flaws,
Prepare yourselves! Behold!"

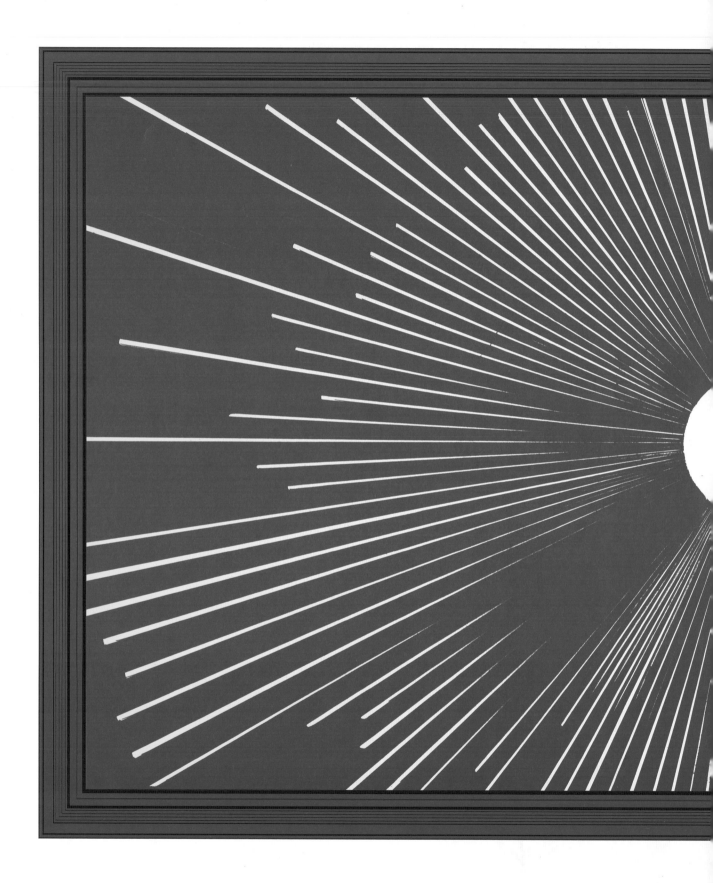

At this, the clouds vanished and the sun lit up the lake. The birds could no longer see their own reflections in the water. All was dazzling light. In this moment of silence when no thoughts of "you" or "me" or "this" or "that" passed before their minds, the birds found themselves in the loving embrace of God, their true King.